the Bruce swap

BY RYAN T. HIGGINS

Disney · HYPERION
Los Angeles   New York

For cousins Karen, Jillian, and Gregory
—who are just the right amount of fun.

First Edition, May 2021 • 10 9 8 7 6 5 4 3 2 1 • FAC-029191-21078 • Printed in Malaysia
This book is set in Macarons/Fontspring; Burbank/House Industries; with additional hand-lettering by Ryan T. Higgins. • Designed by Tyler Nevins
Illustrations were created using scans of treated clayboard for textures, graphite, ink, and Photoshop.

Library of Congress Cataloging-in-Publication Data

Names: Higgins, Ryan T., author, illustrator.
Title: The Bruce swap / by Ryan T. Higgins.
Description: [Los Angeles : Disney-Hyperion, 2021] | Series: Mother Bruce
  | Audience: Ages 3–5. | Audience: Grades K–1. | Summary: Bruce the
  bear's family wishes he were less grumpy, but when his cousin Kevin
  arrives for a visit, he brings more fun than they ever wanted.
Identifiers: LCCN 2020026564 | ISBN 9781368028561 (hardcover)
Subjects: CYAC: Bears—Fiction. | Geese—Fiction. | Mice—Fiction. |
  Behavior—Fiction.
Classification: LCC PZ7.H534962 Bq 2021 | DDC [E]—dc23
LC record available at https://lccn.loc.gov/2020026564
Reinforced binding

Visit www.DisneyBooks.com

JJ
HIGGINS
RYAN

There was a letter in the mailbox
at 13 Go Away Lane.

It was a very fun letter.

The very fun letter was about a very fun visit for Bruce.

Bruce didn't like very fun visits.

And he also didn't like very fun letters.

But he never got to read this one.

Then one day Bruce said no to fun one too many times.

That night, Bruce's family went to bed disappointed.
Each of them made a secret wish.

Thistle secretly wished Bruce
was more cheerful.

Rupert secretly wished Bruce
was more adventurous.

Nibbs secretly wished Bruce
had more pizzazz.

The geese secretly wished
for sandwiches.

Early the next morning, before the first rays of sun crept across Soggy Hollow, Bruce woke up to go on a fishing trip.

Alone.

By himself.

He left a note, of course.

But nobody read that note either.

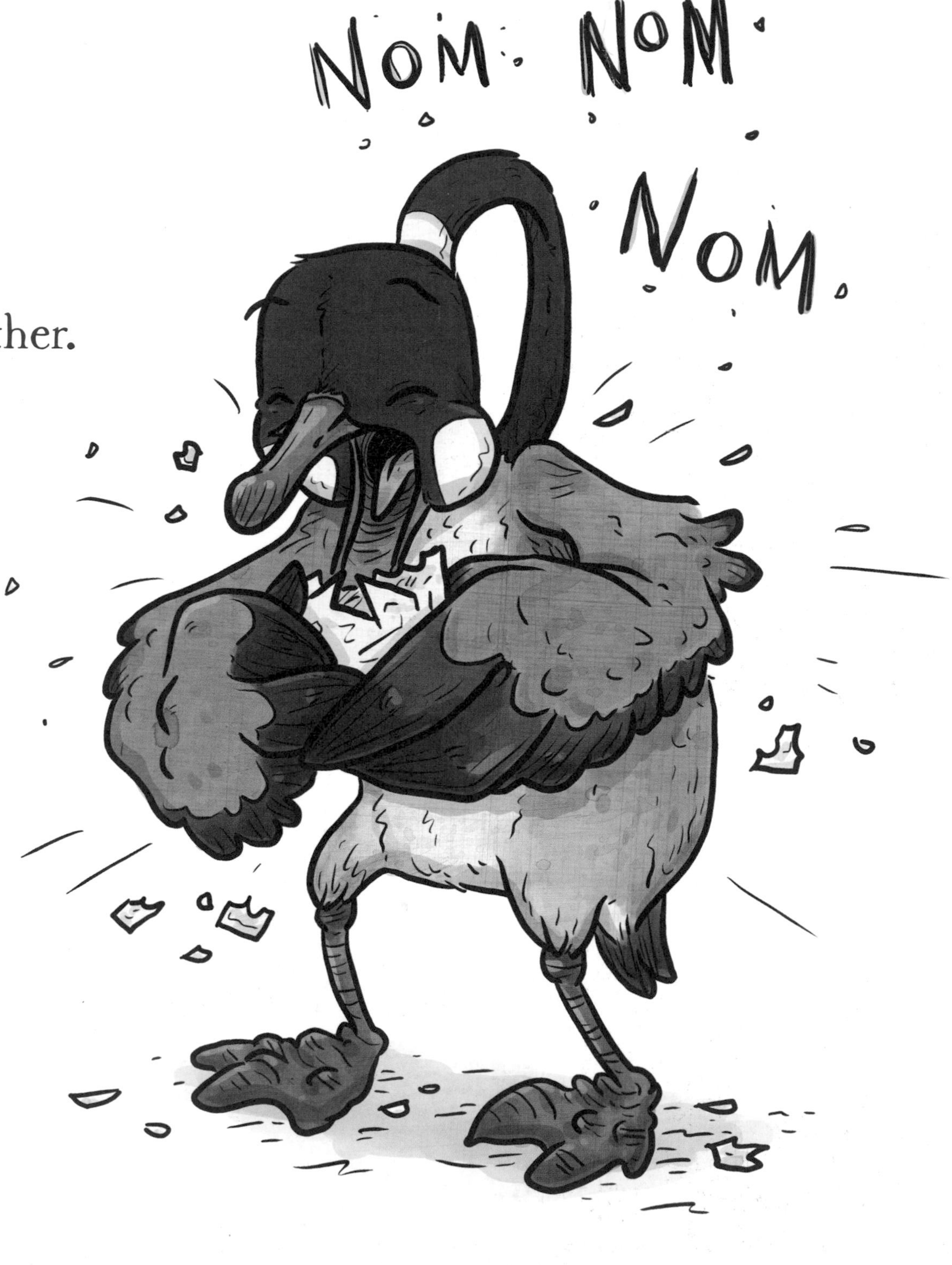

And there he was: Bruce. But not exactly Bruce.
Something was different.

Thistle could see by the
smile on his face that he
was a cheerful bear.

Rupert could see by the
glint in his eye that he
was an adventurous bear.

Nibbs could see by
the bounce in his step
that he was a bear
with pizzazz.

And the geese could
see by his basket of
sandwiches that he
was a bear . . . with
sandwiches.

Rupert said, "Gasp! My wish came true!"

Thistle said, "Squeak! My wish came true, too!"

Nibbs said, "Eeep! My wish came true, too, also!"

The geese . . . ate the sandwiches.

Even with the confusion,
Kevin made friends right away,

because it is fun to make friends
with a friend who is fun.

LET'S EAT CANDY
ALL DAY!
CANDY IS FUN!

And Kevin was
VERY fun.

Hooray!

. . . and coming.

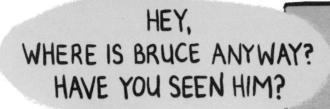

Soon, nobody
was having
any fun
having fun
anymore.

Nibbs and Rupert and Thistle and the geese
wished for the fun to stop.

They all wished for regular Bruce to come back.

WAHHHHHH!

As the fun bus drove out of sight, the roar of its engine faded away.

Quietly, distantly, the grumbly familiar *putt, putt, putt* of a motorbike could be heard.

It was Bruce—the real Bruce and not the one who was actually Kevin—coming home.

Bruce did not know what
had happened that day.

He saw the sad little mice and the pitiful geese
and realized something had to be done.

He decided that maybe . . . just maybe . . .
he should try having FUN.

Bruce's family said no to fun
one too many times.

So Bruce gave up on fun
and took everyone inside.

That's when Bruce saw what
FUN had done to his house.

And Bruce was grumpy again.

Everything was back to normal.

The mice wanted to
hug Bruce all day.

Bruce wanted the
day to be over.

And the geese wanted
more sandwiches.

But they got twenty-six pizzas instead.